The Grand Hotel's Returning Visitor

Karen Evans

Copyright © 2022 Karen Evans

All rights reserved, including the right to reproduce this book, or portions thereof in any form. No part of this text may be reproduced, transmitted, downloaded, decompiled, reverse engineered, or stored, in any form or introduced into any information storage and retrieval system, in any form or by any means, whether electronic or mechanical without the express written permission of the author.

This is a work of fiction. Names and characters are the product of the author's imagination and any resemblance to actual persons, living or dead, is entirely coincidental.

The views expressed in this work are solely those of the author and do not necessarily reflect the views of the publisher, and the publisher hereby disclaims any responsibility for them.

ISBN: 9798812966140

PublishNation
www.publishnation.co.uk

It was the first day in my new job, working on reception at an old Victorian Hotel in Leicester City Centre.

I had often walked past the hotel and admired the grand looking building and always longed to see if the inside was as beautiful as the outside.

It was only by chance that I found out about a receptionists' position becoming available, a customer at the shop I worked at, who was keen to share a good gossip, told me that she had heard the previous receptionist had left quite quickly and no one seemed to know why, my interest piqued, and I made a note to call the hotel the next day to enquire about vacancies

Three weeks later, I took a deep breath and pushed open the main door to the lobby, I looked around and took in the grandeur, I couldn't believe that I had secured such a position

My first week went well and was uneventful, I picked up the system quickly and slotted in well with the team, who were all friendly and welcoming

The hotel was mainly used by business travellers through the week due to the close proximity to the train station as well as nearby offices and the city centre, but it was the weekends when the hotel came alive with balls / parties / weddings and various functions. The grand Kings Hall really lived up to its name with its high ceilings and crystal chandeliers that sparkled in the light. The room was decorated in keeping with its Victorian image but modern enough to feel warm and welcoming

During a show round with the events manager, so that I could get a feel for the hotel in case of any queries, I stepped into the hall immediately getting goosebumps on my arms and a shiver down my back, even though the room itself was comfortably warm, I looked around and took in the atmosphere and immediately felt transported back in time where Ladies were dressed up in beautiful, elegant ballgowns and tiaras, and gentlemen in their black tuxedos and black ties waltzed around the ballroom to the orchestra playing on the stage

"Karen, are you with me so far?" suddenly bringing me back to the present, I turned to Austin "Sorry, I was just taking in the amazing room, its so beautiful. Tell me again the numbers and figures for this amazing room". Finishing the tour of the hotel and the end of my shift, I went to the staff area to get my bag, reaching in to retrieve my phone, I heard a 'thud' behind me, turning around, a picture of the hotel from when it first opened, had come off of the wall and was laying on the floor, with it being such a large picture and given that it had to be drilled onto the wall, I was taken aback as to how it could have come down, nobody else was in the area and I know I hadn't brushed past it, causing it to potentially come free, making a note for the maintenance team for the following day to put it back up, I hoped I wouldn't get into trouble, and felt a shiver as I walked past and out the door

As the weeks past and I got to know the regular guests, my confidence soared and I began to really enjoy the job, no two days were the same and my colleagues became my second family

I was working the late reception when the first of the summer events was taking place in the Kings Hall, I was totally taken aback as to how stunning the hall looked when it was set up. Tonight was the first of many student balls that was taking place with us, how times have changed, back when I was that age, we had a disco at the school hall to mark the end of school, but now it was all proms & balls in posh places with ball gowns and black ties

Feeling the excitement in the air as the events staff bustled about making the final last-minute preparations, I made my way back to reception ready to greet the students and teachers and point them in the right direction of the hall

The evening went on uneventful, and as the last of the party guests left the building, the events staff began the long task of cleaning up ready for the next day. Saying my goodnights on my way out, I noticed a stray dirty plate by the door, picking it up I took it straight to the kitchen, knowing that all the kitchen staff had long gone for the day, I switched on the light and hurried over to the sink, washed the plate and put it safely on the draining board to dry. As I switched out the light, I heard a smash behind me, flicking the light back on, the plate I had just washed was in several pieces on the centre island, puzzled as to how it had got there, I wrapped the broken plate up in kitchen towel and placed it in the bin , as I turned, I shuddered, a cold wave going down my back, figuring I was just tired, I walked to the door and flicked the light off, feeling a cold touch on my arm, I looked round and saw a tall lady with long dark hair wearing a long, elegant white dress, I was about to ask her who she was, when she just vanished right into thin air

Hurrying back to the reception area, the night porter asked if I was ok, saying I looked like I'd just seen a ghost. "just tired that's all" I stammered, and went out the doors into the night and made my way home to bed

The next day, I made the most of the late start and decided to have a good spring clean at home and make the most of the mild weather, having all the windows open and having music playing to dance and sing to, the previous evening long forgotten, when the postman rustled the letterbox, opening a letter from my friend in Scotland, I smiled in delight to read that Cal was able to come for a visit for a few days the following month. Cal and I were pen pals as teenagers and as times changed, we switched to emails, texts and social media to keep in touch, but every now and then we still liked to exchange the odd letter for old times sake, picking up my phone to text Cal to let her know how excited I was for her upcoming visit, I made a note to ask my boss later if we could make use of staff rates for a couple of nights, as I knew Cal would love staying at such a beautiful building

The following weeks went by busily but uneventful, before long Cal's visit was here, I was on the early shift so that I could meet my friend from the train station, Cal is passionate about trains so she would be buzzing from the long trip down from Inverness. Paul checked me into the room at the end of my shift and I took my bag up, figuring I just about had time for a quick shower as the train station is only a 2-minute walk away. Pottering about the room feeling refreshed, my phone sounded a text message from Cal to say that her train was just pulling in, I grabbed my bag and went on up to the station, getting there just as Cal was walking up the steps, waving enthusiastically. Even though we haven't seen each other in so long, it felt like it was only yesterday and we chatted all the way back to the hotel, pushing open the main doors, Cal was taken aback by the grandeur of the lobby, we opted to have a coffee and a sandwich in the lobby bar while we caught up. "ooh this is such good coffee" exclaimed Cal with a smile. She looked around in awe, not believing that she was actually here in such a grand place drinking coffee with her friend after so long of not seeing each other, "I cant wait to see the rest of this amazing place" she smiled

Once we'd finished, we dropped Cal's bags into our room and I gave her a tour of my new place of work, still amazed myself that I had been able to secure a position in such a beautiful place.

Standing in the Kings Hall, Cal suddenly stopped talking mid-sentence and went deathly pale staring up at the balcony, Concerned, I lightly touched her arm and asked if she was ok, bringing her back to the present she shrugged it off and laughed nervously "I'm just tired, it's been a long day", but she just couldn't take her eyes from the balcony, leading my friend out of the room and heading back to the lobby to order more coffee, Cal quickly returned to herself. The afternoon went by quickly and before we knew it, it was time to get ready for dinner, opting to have food ordered to the room so that we could chill in our pyjamas over a bottle of wine with the TV on. Cal had had a long day with an early start, so a quiet evening with an early night was called for

Sound asleep, I was woken up suddenly, Cal was sitting upright and shaking, I put the kettle on to make a hot drink and asked Cal if she'd had a bad dream. "No, I got up to use the bathroom, as I came out, there was a lady in white standing between the two beds, when she saw me, she put her finger up to her lips, then just vanished into thin air, I swear I didn't imagine it" taking the drink that I had made I noticed the change in temperature between the two beds, I shivered noticing goosebumps on my arms and quickly got back under the covers of my own bed and switched on the bedside light. "well, whoever she was, she's gone now" I said, remembering the lady that I had seen in the kitchen when I had first started working at the hotel.

The next day, I showed Cal the sights of my hometown, and we saw a flyer for an historical walk for that evening, so heading off for a quick bite to eat and a sit down first, we enjoyed the stroll around the historical side of the city, taking in the tales of Black Anis, the history of the Guildhall, the cathedral and the story of King Richard the 3rd being found under a local carpark. Back at the hotel, Cal put the kettle on to make hot drinks to warm up, I commented that the walk was a lovely thing to do as sometimes we become oblivious to the history of our own hometown, chatting away, we suddenly heard a 'tap, tap, tap' at the bathroom door, looking up, we both saw the door slam shut! We both jumped up and tentively opened the door, the bath was filling up with hot water and some of Cal's bubble bath had been poured in creating lots of bubbles, trembling, I reached over and switched off the taps, "Well obviously something thinks we smell and needs a bath" I said, which had us both falling about laughing and the tension eased. "well, I was contemplating taking my tea and getting in the bath to warm up, but I'm definitely leaving the door open now," laughed Cal. I pottered about the room while Cal soaked in the bath, pondering what on earth was going on!

The following day was Cal's last day, it was a lovely day so we asked the kitchen to make up a picnic and we headed to nearby Abbey Park for a walk and some peace away from the bustling city centre, before long it was time to make a move ready for Cal to catch her train. Heading back to the hotel first to collect Cal's belongings, Cal asked if she could take another look at the amazing Kings Hall. We had plenty of time so I said that would be fine, I stood back while Cal was again drawn to the Balcony, I could hear her whispering a small prayer, eventually giving a small wave before turning to leave. We then wandered up to the train station and said our goodbyes, vowing to not leave it so long next time. I then wandered back to the hotel to collect my own belongings and check my shifts for that week, Paul enquired after my friends visit and hoped she had a good time. Paul has worked at the hotel for over 20 years and was extremely knowledgeable on the hotel's history, I asked Paul if he had heard of any unusual sightings or goings on, he smiled and said "I wondered how long it would be before you noticed anything". He went on to tell me that the hotel was owned by two spinster sisters, they lived and breathed the hotel and that they often like to make themselves known to new members of staff as they like to make sure that the hotel is still running to their standards. "But the bath started running by itself and even poured bubble bath" I responded, Paul smiled and said "I expect they were just looking out for your friend, as I believe she saw more than she is letting on and they were appreciative of that"

The days and weeks went by quite quickly, I didn't mention what I had learnt to Cal as it was her story to tell of what she felt or saw on the balcony, but felt privileged that the sisters felt protective of my friend

Christmas was coming up, and my Dad and his partner, Pat wanted to book a visit to

Leicester to take in the Christmas market as well as visit family in the area. My dad & Pat live in Cornwall, so asked of they could stay at the hotel they had heard so much about for their visit. We were starting to get busy with Christmas events and Paul had recruited a new receptionist, Anett to help with the extra work, we hit it off immediately and quickly became firm friends, I looked forward to our shifts together as we shared the same sense of humour and love of good coffee. Paul allocated my parents a quiet room and checked them in while I was busy sorting out guests for that nights Christmas party. When I had my break, I used the time to show my Dad & Pat around the hotel, and they were in awe of the Kings Hall all set out for that nights party. Hearing a 'thud' from the balcony, we looked up and saw a shadow move around then disappear, wondering if it was just the lighting, I took my parents down to the restaurant so that they could get dinner while I returned to finish my shift. The next morning I arrived at the hotel early to spend time with my parents. The German Market was in town and we enjoyed looking around, taking in the sights and smells, sampling the wares and having a good catch up. I asked how they liked the room, and caught a quick glance pass between them before Pat replied "its lovely, and our food at dinner was amazing", my dad was unusually quiet, so I put it down to him being tired after such a long drive the day before.

Shopped out, I helped them take their bags back to their room and ordered coffee & sandwiches on room service while Pat sorted out her belongings. My dad decided to soak in the bath, so I took the opportunity to ask if he was ok, she explained that he got up in the night and couldn't get back to sleep so decided to go exploring the hotel and found himself back in the Kings Hall, everyone had gone for the night and he saw a figure of a tall lady dressed in white, jump from the balcony, he ran over but it was like she had just vanished into thin air, so it shook him up a bit. So, I told Pat all about my own experiences of the lady in the kitchen and also what had happened when Cal visited and also my chat with Paul about the two sisters who originally owned the hotel, getting goosebumps despite the warm temperature in the room, suddenly my dad screamed and burst into the room wearing just a towel, white as a sheet and shaking, I guided him to the edge of the bed to sit down, handing him a mug of coffee, my dad eventually calmed down enough to tell us that a lady dressed in white just appeared out of nowhere next to the bath, then turned and walked right through the wall into the bedroom "she looked just like the lady that I saw jump from the balcony last night", "well Shes definitely not here " scolded Pat. So I repeated my own experiences since starting at the hotel as well as what Paul had told me of the two sisters. "don't be daft, there's no such thing as ghosts" my dad laughed, "ok so you just imagined this lady then, did you?" I replied with a raised eyebrow, getting up, my dad returned to the bathroom to get dressed without saying a word.

The rest of their stay was uneventful, my parents managed to catch up with family as well as take in the Christmas sights and shopping. It was my day off when they decided to head home so they called into my house to see the renovations that we had done recently. My dad seemed happier and the colour had returned to his cheeks. "I had a good chat with that manager of yours, Paul, earlier, really nice guy and extremely knowledgeable, the history of that hotel is amazing" my dad informed me "oh and that friend of yours, Anett, has invited me to her wedding" he laughed, I smiled, imagining the conversation Anett would have had with my dad, but deep-down I was glad that my dad liked my new friend as well as my workplace, I had settled there really well and thoroughly enjoyed meeting people from all walks of life, the hours were long and at times unsocial, but I got a buzz from the place that I've never experienced before at work.

Waving my Dad & Pat goodbye and wishing them a great Christmas, I text Anett to say "I hear you're getting married 😊" and enjoyed the rest of my day off curled up with a good book

The next day, I vowed to find out more of the history of the hotel, I went up into the balcony on the Kings Hall to go through some of the boxes of photos that were stored up there. I was drawn to one particular photograph, going cold, the lady looking back at me was the lady that I saw in the kitchen when I was new, turning the card around the name 'Anne' was written in faint ink. Going through more of the photographs, there were lots of shots of the building as it was when it was newly opened, as well as another photo of Anne with another lady who was clearly a relation as they looked so alike. They were handsome ladies but had a sadness to their eyes. I took a photo of these photographs using my phone, to send to Cal and my dad, to see if the ladies resembled who they had seen when they visited. , I was about to close the box up, when I came across a newspaper cutting showing the photo of the two ladies with the headline "Tragedy at the Grand Hotel". I sat down with tears in my eyes to read the article of the two sisters that had run the hotel but had come into financial hardship, they were steeped in debt and couldn't find a way out so made a pact to take their own lives by jumping from the balcony in the Kings Hall, they were discovered in the morning by the early morning cleaner. The hotel lay empty for a couple of years until it was taken over by a hotelier and brought back to its former glory.

Lost in thought and tears streaming down my cheeks, I heard a noise, looking up, I saw the figures of two ladies that waved then vanished just as quickly. Vowing to not let their memory fade, I took the article and the photos to the General Manager and asked If the photos of Anne and her sister could be displayed in the foyer.

As the year came to an end, the photos of the sisters as well as other owners in the hotels history proudly displayed in reception, My dad and Cal both confirmed that it was indeed Anne that they had seen. Anne also started sending me more and more signs that she was around , things that had been misplaced by guests and staff were turning up in the most obscure places

Myself and Anett were working the late shift on New Years eve, which meant we would be seeing in the new year at the hotel, it was a busy evening but we managed to have a good chat and Anett announced that she would like to hold her wedding at the hotel the following year as she had also become fond of Anne and her sister and wanted them to be there for her special day.

As the clock struck midnight, Austin brought us over a glass of fizz each so we could toast the new year too. as I turned to put my glass down, I caught a glimpse of the sisters out of the corner of my eye, they smiled and raised their hands in a wave then vanished into thin air. I smiled as I raised my hand in return and hoped that they were now happy and at peace with how the hotel was evolving.

Printed in Great Britain
by Amazon